JAMES JOYCE

Finnegans Wake

chapter one

THE ILLNESSTRAITED COLOSSICK IDITION

BY **Tim Ahern**

UNIVERSITY OF WASHINGTON PRESS

SEATTLE AND LONDON

Library of Congress Cataloging in Publication Data

Joyce, James, 1882-1941.
    Finnegans wake, chapter 1.

    I. Ahern, Tim. II. Title.
PR6019.O9F52 1983 823'.912   82-20202
ISBN 0-295-95991-6

Introduction

In <u>Finnegans</u> <u>Wake</u>, Joyce's great Mak'nus Op'nus, there is something which peels to the child in us. Much come and tarry has pen bubblished over the ears about the sophisticated languish and hid demeanings defysed by the subtle Irisman. The novel is deaf nitely a goal mind for the scullerly, and it is toutless their efforts which have urned the book its placid twentieth sundry pros.

But Joyce said it's men to make you laugh, and that a child afree could understand it. If Joyce was write, there is only one conclusion: to draw.

Tim Ahern

The text of *Finnegans Wake* reproduced in the following pages is that of pp. 3-29 of the 1958 Viking Press edition in which Joyce's own corrections made shortly before his death are incorporated.

I am grateful to many Joyce scholars for their encouragement during the preparation of this edition, and wish to thank especially Pieter Bekker, Bernard Benstock, Richard Ellmann, Clive Hart, and Harry and Helen Staley. I have learned much from the considerable **Wake** criticism, and hope that its authors will recognize their hand in my drawings.

T. A.

FINNEGANS WAKE

CHAPTER ONE

THE

ILLNESSTRAITED

COLOSSICK

IDITION

riverrun, past Eve and Adam's, from swerve of shore to bend of bay, brings us by a commodius vicus of recirculation back to Howth Castle and Environs.

Sir Tristram,
violer d'amores, fr'over
the short sea, had passen-
core rearrived from North
Armorica on this side the
scraggy isthmus of Europe
Minor to wielderfight his
penisolate war:

nor avoice from afire
bellowsed mishe mishe
to tauftauf thuartpeatrick:
not yet,

nor had topsawyer's rocks
by the stream Oconee ex-
aggerated themselse to
Laurens County's gorgios
while they went doublin
their mumper all the time:

though venissoon after,
had a kidscad buttended
a bland old isaac: not
yet,

though all's fair in
vanessy, were sosie sesthers
wroth with twone nathandjoe.

Rot a peck of pa's malt
had Jhem or Shen brewed
by arclight and rory end
to the regginbrow was
to be seen ringsome on
the aquaface.

The fall

(ba ba ba dal ze hararah ta

ronn konn bronh'oh

tuann thunn

awnska wn too hoo hoor

kamminar

herr onn-
trovarrhoun-

denen thurnuk !:)

of a once wallstrait oldparr
is retaled early in bed and
later on life down through
all christian minstrelsy.

The great fall of the offwall entailed
at such short notice the *pftjschute* of
Finnegan, erse solid man, that the
humptyhillhead of humself prumptly sends
an unquiring one well to the west in
quest of his tumptytumtoes: and their
upturnpikepointandplace is at the knock out
in the park where oranges have been laid
to rust upon the green since devlinsfirst
loved livvy.

What clashes here of wills gen wonts, ostrygods gaggin fishygods! Brékkek Kékkek Kékkek Kékkek! Kóax Kóax Kóax! Ualu Ualu Ualu! Quáouauh! Where the Baddelaries partisans are still out to mathmaster Malachus Micgraines and the Verdons catapelting the camibalistics out of the Whoyteboyce of Hoodie Head. Assiegates and boomeringstroms. Sod's brood, be me fear! Sanglorians, save! Arms appeal with larms, appalling. Killykillkilly: a toll, a toll.

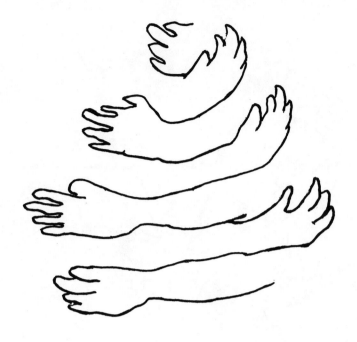

What chance cuddlies, what cashels aired and ventilated! What bidimetoloves sinduced by what tegotetabsolvers! What true feeling for their's hayair with what strawng voice of false jiccup! O here how hoth sprowled met the duskt the father of fornicationists but, (O my shining stars and body!) how hath fanespanned most high heaven the sky-sign of soft advertisement! But waz iz? Iseut? Ere were sewers? The oaks of ald now they lie in peat yet elms leap where askes lay. Phall if you but will, rise you must: and none so soon either shall the pharce for the nunce come to a setdown secular phoenish.

Bygmester Finnegan,

of the Stuttering Hand, freemen's maurer, lived in the broadest way immarginable in his rushlit toofarback for messuages before joshuan judges had given us numbers or Helviticus committed deuteronomy

(one yeastyday he sternely struxk his tete in a tub for to watsch the future of his fates but ere he swiftly stook it out again, by the might of moses, the very water was eviperated and all the guenneses had met their exodus so that ought to show you what a pentschanjeuchy chap he was!)

and during mighty odd years this man
of hod, cement and edifices in Toper's
Thorp piled buildung supra buildung
pon the banks for the livers by the
Soangso.

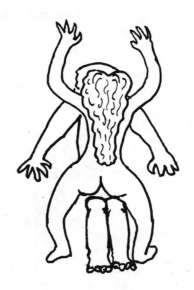

He addle liddle phifie Annie
ugged the little craythur. Wither
hayre in honds tuck up your part
inher.

Oftwhile balbulous, mithre ahead,
with goodly trowel in grasp and ivoroiled
overalls which he habitacularly fondseed,
like Haroun Childeric Eggeberth he would
caligulate by multiplicables the alltitude and
malltitude until he seesaw by neatlight
of the liquor wheretwin 'twas born, his
roundhead staple of other days to rise in
undress maisonry upstanded (joygrantit!), a
waalworth of a skyerscape of most eyeful hoyth
entowerly, erigenating from next to nothing and
celescalating the himals and all, hierarchitectitip-
titoploftical, with a burning bush abob off its
baubletop and with larrons o' toolers clittering up and
tombles a' buckets clottering down.

Of the first was he to bare
arms and a name: Wassaily Boos-
laeugh of Riesengeborg. His crest
of huroldry, in vert with ancillars,
troublant, argent, a hegoak, poursuivant,
horrid, horned. His scutschum fessed,
with archers strung, helio, of the second.

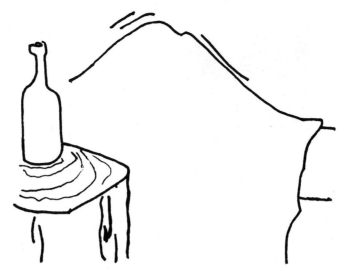

Hootch is for husbandman handling his hoe.
Hohohoho, Mister Finn, you're going to be
Mister Finnagain! Comeday morm and O, you're
vine! Sendday's eve and, ah, you're vinegar!
Hahahaha, Mister Funn, you're going to be
fined again!

What then agentlike brought about that tragoady
thundersday this municipal sin business? Our cubehouse still
rocks as earwitness to the thunder of his arafatas but we
hear also through successive ages that shebby choruysh of un-
kalified muzzlenimiissilehims that would blackguardise the
whitestone ever hurtleturtled out of heaven.

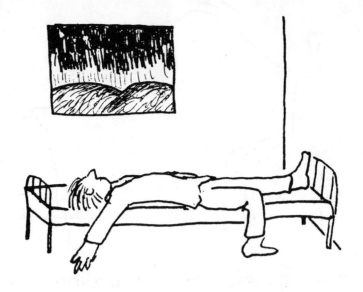

Stay us wherefore in our search for
tighteousness, O Sustainer, what time we
rise and when we take up to toothmick and
before we lumpdown upown our leatherbed
and in the night and at the fading of the stars!
For a nod to the nabir is better than wink to the
wabsanti.

Otherways wesways like that provost scoffing
bedoueen the jebel and the jpysian sea. Cropherb
the crunchbracken shall decide. Then we'll know
if the feast is a flyday. She has a gift of seek
on site and she allcasually ansars helpers, the
dreamydeary.

Heed! Heed!

It may half been a missfired brick,
as some say, or it mought have been
due to a collupsus of his back promises,
as others looked at it. (There extand by
now one thousand and one stories, all told,
of the same). But so sore did abe ite
ivvy's holired abbles (what with the
wallhall's horrors of rollsrights, carhacks,
stonengens, kisstvanes, tramtrees,
fargobawlers, autokinotons, hippo-
hobbilies, streetfleets, tournintaxes,
megaphoggs, circuses and wardsmoats,
basilikerks and aeropagods and
the hoyse and the jollybrool and
the peeler in the coat and the
mecklenburk bitch bite at his ear
and the merlinburrow burrocks
and his fore old porecourts,
the bore the more, and his blightblack
workingstacks at twelvepins a dozen
and the noobibusses sleighding along
Safetyfirst Street and the derryjellybies
snooping around Tell-No-Tailors' Corner
and the fumes and the hopes and the
strupithump of his ville's indigenous
romekeepers, homesweepers, dome-
creepers, thurum and thurum in
fancymud murumd and all the uproar
from all the aufroofs, a roof for
  may and a reef for hugh butt
under his bridge suits tony)

wan warning Phill
filt tippling full.
His howd feeled
heavy, his hoddit
did shake.
(There was a
wall of course
in erection)

Dimb!
He stottered from
the latter.

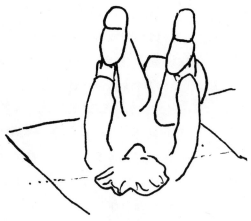

Damb!
He was dud.

Mastabatoom, mastabadtomm, when a mon merries his lute is all long. For whole the world to see.

Shize? I should shee! Macool, Macool, orra whyi deed ye diie?

Sobs they sighdid at Fillagain's chrissormiss wake, all the hoolivans of the nation, prostrated in their consternation and their duodisimally profusive plethora of ululation. There was plumbs and grumes and cheriffs and citherers and raiders and cineman too. And the all gianed in with the shoutmost shoviality. Agog and magog and the round of them agrog. To the continuation of that celebration until Handand hunigan's extermination! Some in kinkin corass, more, kankan keening. Belling him up and filling him down. He's stiff but he's steady is Priam Olim! 'Twas he was the dacent gaylabouring youth. Sharpen his pillowscone, tap up his bier! E'erawhere in this whorl would ye hear such a din again? With their deepbrow fundigs and the dusty fidelios. They laid him brawdawn alanglast bed. With a bockalips of finisky fore his feet. And a barrowload of guenesis hoer his head.

Tee the tootal of the fluid hang the twoddle of the fuddled, O'!

Hurrah, there is but young gleve for the owl globe wheels in view which is tautaulogically the same thing.

Well, him a being so on the flounder of his bulk like an overgrown babeling, let wee peep, see, at Hom, well, see peegee ought he ought, platterplate. [I] Hum! From Shopalist to Baily-wick or from ashtun to baronoath or

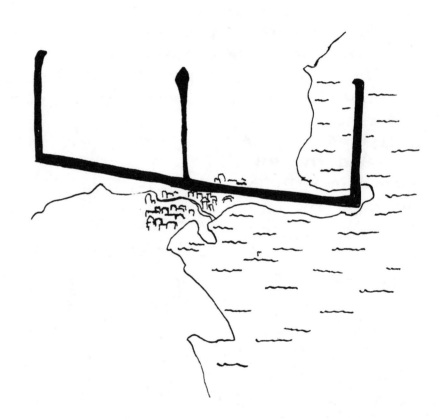

from Buythebanks to Roundthehead or from the foot of the bill to ireglint's eye he calmly extensolies.

And all the way (a horn!) from fjord to fjell his baywinds' oboboes shall wail him rockbound (hoahoahoah!) in swimswamswum and all the livvylong night, the delldale dallpling night, the night of bluerybells, her flittaflute in tricky trochees (O carina! O carina!) wake him.

With her issavan essavans and her patterjackmartins about all them inns and ouses. Tilling a teel of a tum, telling a toll of a teary turty Taubling.

Grace before Glutton. For what we are, gifs à gross if we are, about to believe. So pool the begg and pass the kish for crawsake. Omen. So sigh us. Grampupus is fallen down but grinny sprids the boord. Whase on the joint of a desh? Finfoefom the Fush. Whase be his baken head? A loaf of Singpantry's Kennedy bread. And whase hitched to the hop in his tayle? A glass of Danu U' Dunnell's foamous olde Dobbelin ayle. But, lo, as you would quaffoff his fraudstuff and sink teeth through that pyth of a flowerwhite bodey behold of him as behemoth for he is noewhemoe.

Finiche! Only a fadograph of a
yestern scene. Almost rubicund
Salmosalar, ancient fromout the ages
of the Agapemonides, he is smolten
in our mist, woebecanned and packt
away. So that meal's dead off for summan,
schlook, schlice and goodridhirring.

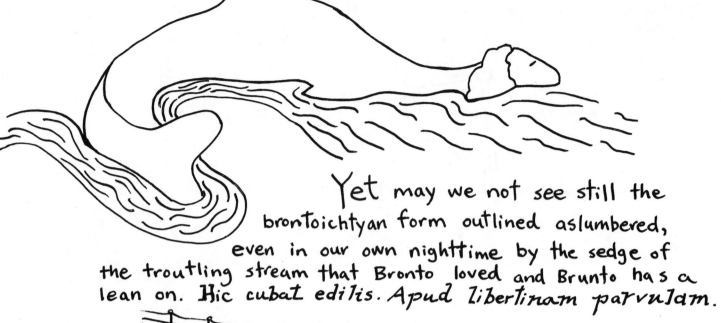

Yet may we not see still the brontoichtyan form outlined aslumbered, even in our own nighttime by the sedge of the troutling stream that Bronto loved and Brunto has a lean on. *Hic cubat edilis. Apud libertinam parvulam.*

Whatif she be in flags or flitters, reekierags or sundyechosies, with a mint of mines or beggar a punnyweight. Arrah, sure, we all love little Anny Ruiny, or, we mean to say, lovelittle Anny Rayiny, when unda her brella, mid piddle med puddle, she ninnygoes nannygoes nancing by.

Yoh! Brontolone slaaps, yoh snoores. Upon Benn Heather, in Seeple Isout too. The cranic head on him, caster of his reasons, peer yuthner in yondmist.

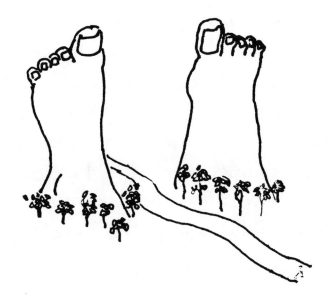

Whooth? His clay feet, swarded in verdigrass, stick up starck where he last fellonem, by the mund of the magazine wall, where our maggy seen all, with her sisterin shawl.

While over against this belles' alliance beyind
Ill Sixty, ollollowed ill! bagsides of the fort, bom,
tarabom, tarabom, lurk the ombushes, the site of the
lyffing-in-wait of the upjock and hockums. Hence when
the clouds roll by, jamey, a proudseye view is
enjoyable of our mounding's mass, now Wallinstone
national museum, with, in some greenish distance,
the charmful waterlooge country and the two quite-
white villagettes who hear show of themselves so
gigglesomes minxt the follyages, the prettilees!

Penetrators are permitted into the museomound free. Welsh and the Paddy Patkinses, one shelenk! Redismembers invalids of old guard find poussepousse pousseypram to sate the sort of their butt. For her passkey supply to the janitrix, the mistress Kathe. Tip.

This is the way to the museyroom.
Mind your hats goan in !

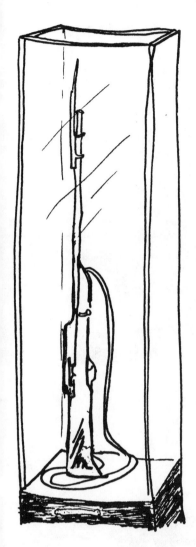

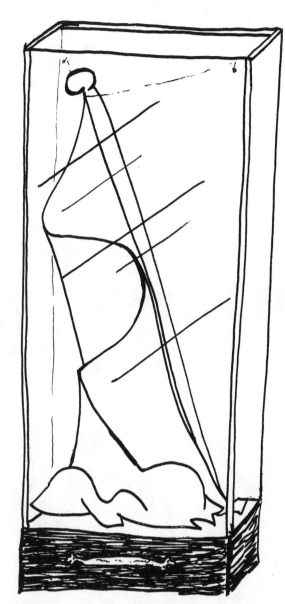

Now yiz are in
the Willingdone
Museyroom. This
is a Prooshious
gunn. This is a
ffrinch.

Tip.

This is the flag
of the Prooshious,
the Cap and Soracer.

This is the
bullet that
byng the
flag of the
Prooshious.

This is the ffrinch that fire on the Bull that byng the flag of the Prooshious. Saloos the Crossgunn! Up with your pike and fork! Tip. (Bullsfoot! Fine!)

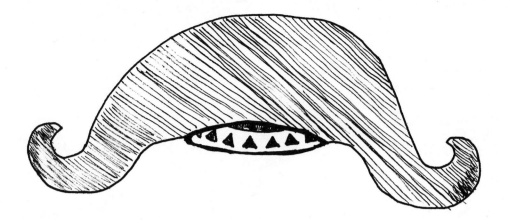

This is the triplewon hat of Lipoleum. Tip. Lipoleumhat.

This is the Willingdone on his same white harse, the Cokenhape. This is the big Sraughter Willingdone, grand and magentic in his goldtin spurs and his ironed dux and his quarterbrass woodyshoes and his magnate's gharters and his bangkok's best and goliar's goloshes and his pulluponeasyan wartrews. This is his big wide harse.

This is the three lipoleum boyne grouching down in the living detch. This is an inimyskilling inglis, this is a scotcher grey, this is a davy, stooping. This is the bog lipoleum mordering the lipoleum beg. A Gallawghurs argaument. This is the pretty lipoleum boy that was nayther bag nor bug. Assaye, assaye! Touchole Fitz Tuomush. Dirty MacDyke. And Hairy O'Hurry. All of them arminus-varminus.

This is Delian alps. This is Mont Tivel, this is Mont Tipsey, this is the Grand Mons Injun. This is the crimealine of the alps hooping to sheltershock the three lipoleums.

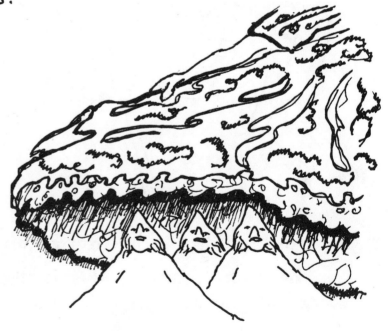

This is the jinnies with their legahorns feinting to read in their handmade's book of stralegy while making their war undisides the Willingdone. The jinnies is a cooin her hand and the jinnies is a ravin her hair and the Willingdone git the band up.

This is big Willingdone mormorial tallowscoop Wounderworker obscides on the flanks of the jinnies. Sexcaliber hrosspower. Tip.

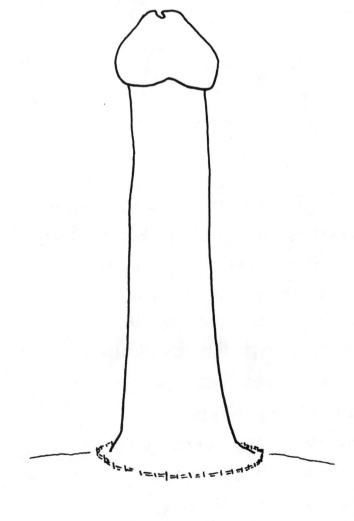

This is me Belchum sneaking his phillipy out of his most Awful Grimmest Sunshat Cromwelly. Looted.

Lieber Arthur, wir siegen! Wie geht's deiner Kleinen Frau? Hochachtung,
     -Nap

This is the jinnies' hastings dispatch for to irrigate the Willingdone. Dispatch in thin red lines cross the shortfront of me Belchum. Yaw, yaw, yaw! Leaper Orthor. Fear siecken! Fieldgaze thy tiny frow. Hug-acting. Nap. That was the tictacs of the jinnies for to fontannoy the Willingdone. Shee, shee, shee!

The jinnies is jillous agin-courting all the lipoleums. And the lipoleums is gonn boy-cottoncrazy onto the one Willingdone. And the Willingdone git the band up. This is bode Belchum, bonnet to busby, breaking his secred word with a ball up his ear to the Willingdone.

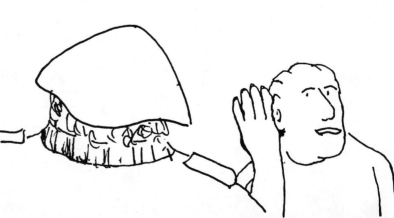

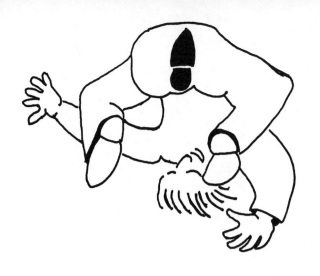

This is the Willingdone's hurold dispitchback. Dispitch desployed on the regions rare of me Belchum. Salamangra! Ayi, ayi, ayi! Cherry jinnies. Figtreeyou! Damn fairy ann, Voutre. Willingdone. That was the first joke of Willingdone, tic for tac. Hee, hee, hee!

This is me Belchum in his twelve mile cowchooks, weet, tweet and stampforth foremost, footing the camp for the jinnies. Drink a sip, drankasup, for he's as sooner buy a guinness than he'd stale store stout. This is Rooshious balls. This is a ttrinch. This is mistletropes. This is Canon Futter with the popynose. After his hundred days' indulgence. This is the blessed. Tarra's widdars! This is jinnies in the bonny bawn blooches. This is lipoleums in the rowdy howses. This is the Willingdone, by the splinters of Cork, order fire. Tonnerre! (Bullsear! Play!) This is camelry, this is floodens, this is the solphereens in action, this is their mobbily, this is panickburns. Almeidagad! Arthiz too loose! This is Willingdone cry. Brum! Brum! Cumbrum!

This is jinnies cry. Underwetter! Goat strip Finnlambs!
This is jinnies rinning away to ther ousterlists dowan a
bunkersheels. With a nip nippy nip and a trip trippy trip so
airy. For their heart's right there. Tip. This is me Belchum's
tinkyou tankyou silvoor plate for citchin the crapes in the
cool of his canister. Poor the pay! This is the bissmark of
the marathon merry of the jinnies they left behind them. This
is the Willingdone branlish his same marmorial tallowscoop
Sophy - Key - Po for his royal divorsion on the rinnaway
jinnies. Gambariste della porca! Dalaveras fimmieras!

This is the pettiest of the
lipoleums, Toffeethief, that
spy on the Willingdone from
his big white harse, the Cape-
inhope. Stonewall Willingdone
is an old maxy montrumeny.
Lipoleums is nice hung bushellors.
This is hiena hinnessy laughing
alout at the Willingdone. This
is lipsyg dooley krieging the funk
from the hinnessy. This is the hinndoo Shimar Shin between the
dooley boy and the hinnessy.
Tip.

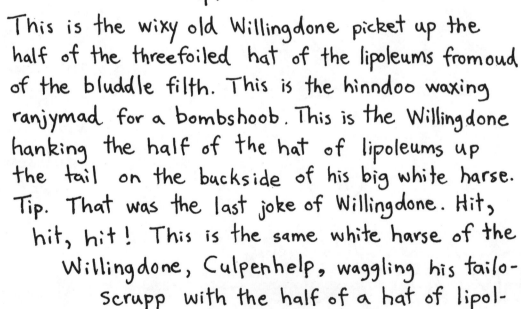

This is the wixy old Willingdone picket up the
half of the threefoiled hat of the lipoleums fromoud
of the bluddle filth. This is the hinndoo waxing
ranjymad for a bombshoob. This is the Willingdone
hanking the half of the hat of lipoleums up
the tail on the buckside of his big white harse.
Tip. That was the last joke of Willingdone. Hit,
hit, hit! This is the same white harse of the
Willingdone, Culpenhelp, waggling his tailo-
scrupp with the half of a hat of lipoleums to insoult on the hinndoo
seeboy. Hney, hney, hney!
(Bullsrag! Foul!)

This is the seeboy, madras-hattaras, upjump and pumpim, cry to the Willingdone, born-stable ghentleman, tinders his maxbotch to the cursigan Shimar Shin. Basucker youstead !

This is the dooforhim seeboy blow the whole of the half of the hat of lipoleums off of the top of the tail on the back of his big wide harse. Tip (Bullseye ! Game !) How Copenhagen ended.

This way the museyroom. Mind your boots goan out.

Phew!
   What a warm time
we were in there but how
keling is here the airabouts!
We nowhere she lives but you mussna
tell annaone for the lamp of Jig-a-Lanthern! It's
a candlelittle houthse of a month and one windies.
Downadown, High Downadown. And numbered quaintly mine.
And such reasonable weather too! The wagrant wind's awalt'
zaround the piltdowns and on every blasted knollyrock (if you
can spot fifty I spy four more) there's that gnarlybird ygathering,
a runalittle, doalittle, preealittle, pouralittle, wipealittle,
kicksalittle, severalittle, eatalittle, whinealittle, kenalittle,
helfalittle, pelfalittle gnarlybird. A verytableland of bleakbardfields!
Under his seven wrothschields lies one, Lumproar. His glav toside
him. Our pigeons pair are flewn for northcliffs.

The three of crows have flapped it southenly, kraaking of de baccle to the kvarters of that sky whence triboos answer; Wail, 'tis well! She niver comes out when Thon's on shower or when Thon's flash with his Nixy girls or when Thon's blowing toomcracks down the gaels of Thon. No nubo no! Neblas on you liv! Here would be too moochy afreet. Of burymeleg and Bindmerollingeyes and all the deed in the woe. Fe fo fom! She jist does hopes till byes will be byes. Here, and it goes on to appear now, she comes, a peacefugle, a parody's bird, a peri potmother, a pringlpik in the ilandiskippy, with peewee and powwows in beggybaggy on her bickybacky and a flick flask fleckflinging its pixylighting pacts' huemeramy- bows, picking here, pecking there, pussypussy plunderpussy. But it's the armitides toonigh, militopucos, and toomourn we wish for a muddy kissmans to the minutia workers and there's to be a gorgeups truce for happinest childher everwere. Come nebo me and suso sing the day we sallybright. She's burrowed the coacher's

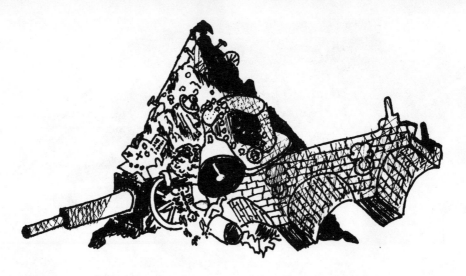

headlight the better to pry (who goes cute goes siocur and shoos aroun) and all spoiled goods go into her nabsack: curtrages and rattlin buttins, nappy spattees and flasks of all nations, clavicures and scampulars, maps, keys and wood-piles of haypennies and moonled brooches with bloodstaned breeks in em, boaston nightgarters and masses of shoesets and nickelly nacks and foder allmichael and a lugly parson of cates and howitzer muchears and midgers and maggets, ills and ells with loffs of toffs and pleures of bell and the last sigh that come fro the hart (bucklied!) and the fairest sin the sunsaw (that's cearc!). With Kiss. Kiss Criss. Cross Criss. Kiss Cross. Undo lives 'end. Slain.

How bootifull and how true-towife of her, when strengly fore-bidden, to steal our historic presents from the past postpropheticals so as to make us all lordy heirs and ladymaidesses of a pretty nice kettle of fruit. She is livving in our midst of debt and laffing

through all plores for us (her birth is uncontrollable), with a naperon for her mask and her sabboes kickin arias (so sair! so solly!) if yous ask me and I saack you. Hou! Hou! Gricks may rise and Troysirs fall (there being two sights for ever a picture) for in the byways of high improvidence that's what makes lifework leaving. and the world's a cell for citters to cit in. Let young wimman run away with the story and let young min talk smooth behind the butteler's back. She knows her knight's duty while Luntum sleeps. Did ye save any tin? says he. Did I what? with a grin says she. And we all like a marriedann because she is mercenary. Though the length of the land lies under liquidation (floote!) and there's nare a hairbrow nor an eyebush on this glaubrous phace of Herrschuft Whatarwelter she'll loan a vesta and hire some peat and sarch the shores her cockles to heat and she'll do all a turfwoman can to piff the business on. Paff. To puff the blaziness on.

Poffpoff. And even if Humpty shell fall frumpty times as awkward again in the beardsboosoloom of all our grand remonstrancers there'll be iggs for the brekkers come to mournhim, sunny side up with care. So true is it that there where's a turnover the tay is wet too and when you think you ketch sight of a hind make sure but you're cocked by a hin.

Then as she is on her behaviourite job of quainance bandy, fruting for firstlings and taking her tithe, we may take our review of the two mounds to see nothing of the himples here as at elsewhere, by sixes and sevens, like so many heegills and collines, sitton aroont, scentbreeched and somepotreek, in their swishawish satins and their taffetaffe tights, playing Wharton's Folly, at a treepurty on the planko in the purk. Stand up, mickos! Make strake for minnas! By order, Nicholas Proud. We may see and hear nothing if we choose of the shortlegged bergins off Corkhill or the bergamoors of Arbourhill or the berga gambols of Summerhill or the bergincellies of Miseryhill or the country-bossed bergones of Constitutionhill though every crowd has its several tones and every trade has its clever mechanics and each harmonical has a point of its own, Olaf's on the rise and Ivor's on the lift and Sitric's place's between them. But all they are all there scraping along to sneeze out a likelihood that will solve and salve life's robulus rebus, hopping round his middle like kippers on a griddle, O, as he lays dormont from the macroborg of Holdhard to the micro-birg of Pied de Poudre. Behove this sound of Irish sense. Really? Here English might be seen. Royally? One sovereign punned to petery pence. Regally? The silence speaks the scene. Fake!

So This Is Dyoublong?

Hush! Caution! Echoland!

How charmingly exquisite! It reminds you of the outwashed engravure that we used to be blurring on the blotch wall of his innkempt house. Used they? (I am sure that chabelshoveller with the mujikal chocolat box, Miry Mitchel, is listening) I say, the remains of the outworn gravemure where used to be blurried the Ptollmens of the Incabus. Used we? (He is only pretendant to be stugging at the jubalee harp from a second existed lishener, Fiery Farrelly.) It is well known. Lokk for himself and see the old butte new. Dbln. W.K.O.O. Hear? By the mausolime wall. Fimfim fimfim. With a grand funferall. Fumfum fumfum. 'Tis optophone with ontophanes. List! Wheatstone's magic lyer. They will be tuggling foriver. They will be lichening for allof. They will be pretumbling forover. The harpsdischord shall be theirs for ollaves.

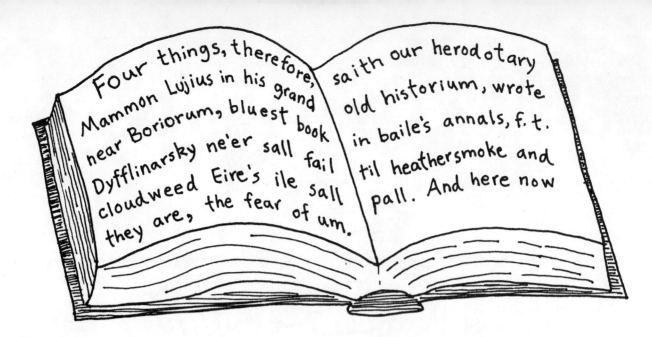

Four things, therefore, saith our herodotary
Mammon Lujius in his grand old historium, wrote
near Boriorum, bluest book in baile's annals, f.t.
Dyfflinarsky ne'er sall fail til heathersmoke and
cloudweed Eire's ile sall pall. And here now
they are, the fear of um.

T. Totities!
Unum. (Adar.)

Ay, ay!
Duum. (Nizam.)

Ah, ho!
Triom. (Tamuz.)

Adear, adear!
Quodſibus.
(Marchessvan.)

A bulbenboss sur-
mounted upon an
alderman.

A shoe on a
puir old wobban.

An auburn mayde,
o'brine a'bride,
to be desarted.

A penn no
weightier nor a
polepost.

And so. And all. (Succoth.)

So, how idlers' wind turning pages on pages, as
innocens with anaclete play popeye antipop, the leaves
of the living in the boke of the deeds, annals of
themselves timing the cycles of events grand and
national, bring fassilwise to pass how.

1132 A.D.

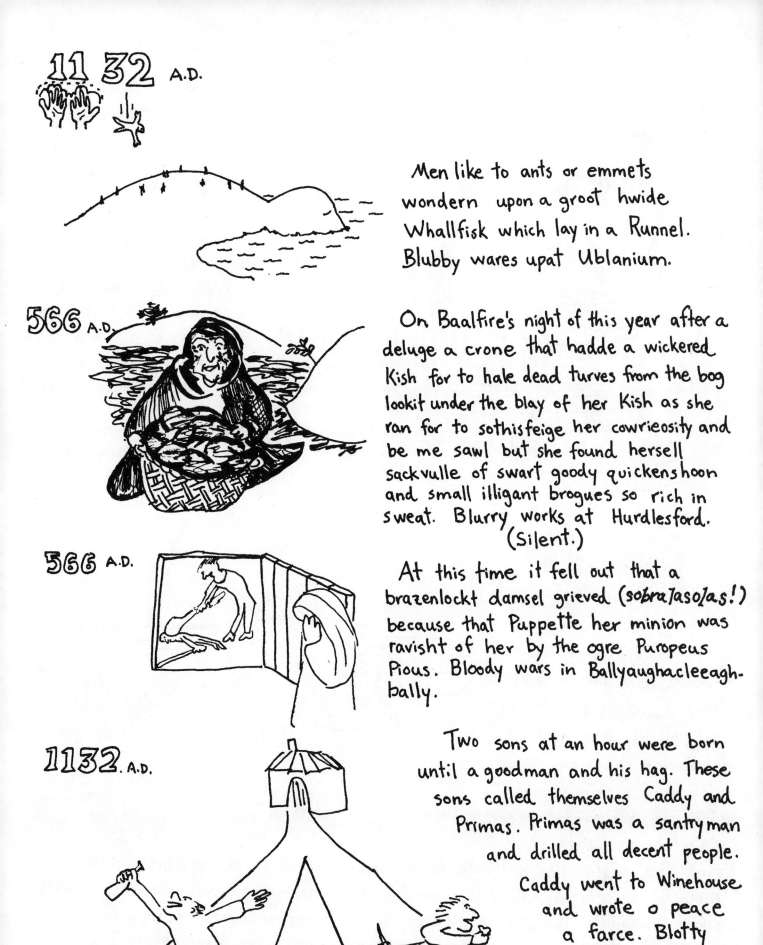

Men like to ants or emmets wondern upon a groot hwide Whallfisk which lay in a Runnel. Blubby wares upat Ublanium.

566 A.D.

On Baalfire's night of this year after a deluge a crone that hadde a wickered Kish for to hale dead turves from the bog lookit under the blay of her Kish as she ran for to sothisfeige her cowrieosity and be me sawl but she found hersell sackvulle of swart goody quickenshoon and small illigant brogues so rich in sweat. Blurry works at Hurdlesford.
(Silent.)

566 A.D.

At this time it fell out that a brazenlockt damsel grieved (*sobra/aso/as!*) because that Puppette her minion was ravisht of her by the ogre Puropeus Pious. Bloody wars in Ballyaughacleeagh-bally.

1132 A.D.

Two sons at an hour were born until a goodman and his hag. These sons called themselves Caddy and Primas. Primas was a santryman and drilled all decent people. Caddy went to Winehouse and wrote o peace a farce. Blotty words for Dublin.

Somewhere, parently, in the ginn-andgo gap between antediluvious and annadominant the copyist must have fled with his scroll. The billy flood rose or an elk charged him or the sultrup worldwright from the excelsissimost empyrean (bolt, in sum) earthspake or the Dannamen gallous banged pan the bliddy duran. A scribicide then and there is led off under old's code with some fine covered by six marks or ninepins in metalmen for the sake of his labour's dross while it will be only now and again in our rear of o'er era, as an upshoot of military and civil engagements, that a gynecure was let on to the scuffold for taking that same fine sum covertly by meddlement with the drawers of his neighbour's safe.

Now after all that farfatch'd and peragrine or dingnant or clere lift we our ears, eyes of the darkness, from the tome of *Liber Lividus* and (toh!), how paisibly eirenical, all dimmering dunes and gloamering glades, selfstretches afore us our fredeland's plain! Lean neath stone

pine the pastor lies with his crook; young pricket by pricket's sister nibbleth on returned viridities; amaid her rocking grasses the herb trinity shams lowliness; skyup is of evergrey. Thus too for donkeys' years. Since the bouts of Hebear and Hairyman the cornflowers have been staying at Ballymun, the duskrose has choosed out Goatstown's hedges, twolips have pressed togatherthem by sweet Rush, townland of twinedlights, the whitehorn and the redthorn have fairygeyed the mayvalleys of Knockmaroon, and, though for rings round them, during a chiliad of perihelygangs, the Formoreans have brittled the tooath of the Danes and the Oxman has been pestered by the Firebugs and the Joynts have thrown up jerrybuilding to the Kevanses and Little on the Green is childfather to the City (Year! Year! And laughtears!), these paxsealing buttonholes have quadrilled across the centuries and whiff now whafft to us, fresh and made-of-all-smiles as, on the eve of Killallwho.

The babbelers with their thangas vain have been (confusium hold them!) they were and went; thigging thugs were and houhnhymn songtoms were and comely norgels were and polyfool fiansees. Men have thawed, clerks have surssurhummed, the blond has sought of the brune:

Elsekiss though may, mean Kerry piggy?: and the duncledames have countered with the hellish fellows: Who ails tongue coddeau, aspace of dumbillsilly?

And they fell upong one another: and themselves they have fallen. And still nowanights and by nights of yore do all bold floras of the field to their shyfawn lovers say only: Cull me ere I wilt to thee!: and but a little later: Pluck me whilst I blush! Well may they wilt, marry, and profusedly blush, be troth! For that saying is as old as the howitts. Lave a whale a while in a whillbarrow (isn't it the truath I'm tallin ye?) to have fins and flippers that shimmy and shake. Tim Timmycan timped hir, tampting Tam. Fleppety! Flippety! Fleapow!

Hop!
In the name of Anem this Carl on the kopje in pelted thongs a parth a lone who the joebiggar be he? Forshapen his pigmaid hoagshead, shroonk his plodsfoot. He hath lockfoes, this shortshins, and, Obeold that's pectoral, his mammamuscles most mousterious. It is slaking nuncheon out of some thing's brain pan. Me seemeth a dragon man. He is almonthst on the kiep fief by here, is Comestipple Sacksoun, be it junipery or febrewery, marracks or alebrill or the ramping riots of pouriose and froriose. What a quhare soort of a mahan. It is evident the michindaddy. Lets we overstep his fire defences and these kraals of slitsucked marogbones (Cave!) He can prapsposterus the pillory way to Hirculos pillar. Come on, fool porterfull, hosiered women blown monk sewer?

Scuse us chorley guy!
You tollerday donsk?   N.
You tolkatiff scowegian? Nn.
You spigotty anglease? Nnn.
You phonio saxo?   Nnnn.
Clear all so! 'Tis a Jute.
Let us swop hats and excheck a few strong verbs weak oach eather yapyazzard abast the blooty creeks.

Jute: — Yuttah!

Mutt. — Mukk's pleasurad.

Jute. — Are you jeff?

Mutt. — Somehards.

Jute. — But you are not jeffmute?

Mutt. — Noho. Only an utterer.

Jute. — Whoa? Whoat is the mutter with you?

Mutt. — I became a stun a stummer.

Jute. — What a hauhauhauhaudibble thing, to be cause! How, Mutt?

Mutt. — Aput the buttle, surd.

Jute. — Whose poddle? Wherein?

Mutt. — The Inns of Dungtarf where Used awe to be he.

Jute. — You that side your voise are almost inedible to me. Become a bitskin more wiseable as if I were you.

Mutt. — Has? Has at? Hasatency? Urp, Boohooru! Booru Usurp! I trumple from rath in mine mines when I rimimirim!

Jute. — One eyegonblack. Bisons is bisons. Let me fore all your hasitancy cross your qualm with trink gilt. Here have sylvan coyne, a piece of oak. Ghinees hies good for you.

Mutt. — Louee, louee! How wooden I not know it, the intellible greytcloak of Cedric Silkyshag! Cead mealy faulty rices for one dabblin bar. Old grilsy growlsy! He was poached on that eggtentical spot. Here where the liveries, Monomark. There where the missers moony, Minnikin passe.

Jute. — Simply because as Taciturn pretells, our wrongstoryshortener, he dumptied the wholeborrow of rubbages on to soil here.

Mutt. — Just how a puddinstone inate the brookcells by a riverpool.

Jute. — Load Allmarshy! Wid wad for a norse like?

Mutt. — Somular with a bull on a clompturf. Rooks roarum rex roome! I could snore to him of the spumy horn,

with his woolseley side in, by the neck I am sutton on, did Brian d' of Linn.

Jute. — Boildoyle and rawhoney on me when I can beuraly forsstand a weird from sturk to finnic in such a patwhat as your rutterdamrotter. Onheard of and umscene! Gut aftermeal! See you doomed.

Mutt — Quite agreem. Bussave a sec. Walk a dun blink round-ward this albutisle and you skull see how olde ye plaine of my Elters, hunfree and ours, where wone to wail whimbrel to peewee o'er the saltings, where wilby citie by law of isthmon, where by a droit of signory, icefloe was from his Inn the Byggning to whose Finishthere Punct. Let erehim ruhmuhrmuhr. Mearmerge two races, swete and brack. Morthering rue. Hither, craching eastuards, they are in surgence: hence, cool at ebb, they requiesce. Countlessness of livestories have netherfallen by this plage, flick as flowflakes, litters from aloft, like a waast wizzard all of whirlwords. Now are all tombed to the mound, isges to isges, erde from erde. Pride, O pride, thy prize!

Jute. — 'Stench!

Mutt. — Fiatfuit! Hereinunder lyethey. Llarge by the smal an' everynight life olso th'estrange, babylone the greatgrand-hotelled with tit tit tittlehouse, alp on earwig, drukn on ild, likeas equal to anequal in this sound seemetery which iz leebez luv.

Jute. — 'Zmorde!

Mutt. — Meldundleize! By the fearse wave behoughted. Despond's sung. And thanacestross mound have swollup them all. This ourth of years is not save brickdust and being humus the same roturns. He who runes may rede it on all fours. O'c'stle, n'wc'stle, tr'c'stle, crumbling! Sell me sooth the fare for Humblin! Humblady Fair. But speak it allsosiftly, moulder! Be in your whisht!

Jute. — Whysht?

Mutt. — The gyant Forficules with Amni the fay.

Jute. — Howe?

Mutt. — Here is viceking's graab.

Jute. — Hwaad!

Mutt. — Ore you astoneaged, jute you?

Jute. — Oye am thonthorstrok, thing mud.

Stoop) if you are abcedminded, to this claybook, what curios of signs (please stoop), in this allaphbed! Can you rede (since We and Thou had it out already) its world? It is the same told of all. Many. Miscegenations on miscegenations. Tieckle. They lived und laughed ant loved end left. Forsin. Thy thingdome is given to Meades and Porsons. The meandertale, aloss and again, of our old Heidenburgh in the days when Head-in-Clouds walked the earth. In the ignorance that implies impression that knits knowledge that finds the nameform that whets the wits that convey contacts that sweeten sensation that drives desire that adheres to attachment that dogs death that bitches birth that entails the ensuance of existentiality. But with a rush out of his navel reaching the reredos of Ramasbatham. A terricolous hinelyonniew this; queer and it continues to be quaky. A hatch, a celt, an earshare the pourquose of which was to cassay the earthcrust at all of hours, furrowards, bagawards, like yoxen at the turnpaht. Here say figurines billy-coose arming and mounting. Mounting and arming bellicose figurines see here. Futhorc, this little effingee is for a firefing called a flintforfall. Face at the eased! O I fay! Face at the waist! Ho, you fie! Upwap and dump em, Tace to Tace! When a part so ptee does duty for the holos we soon grow to use of an allforabit. Here (please to stoop) are selveran cued peteet peas of quite a pecuniar interest inaslittle as they are the pellets that make the Tomtummy's pay roll. Right rank ragnar rocks and with these rox orangotangos rangled rough and rightgorong. Wisha wisha whydidtha? Thik is for thorn that's thuck in its thoil like thumfool's thraitor thrust for vengeance. What a mnice old mness it all mnakes! A middenhide hoard of objects! Olives, beets, kimmells, dollies, alfrids, beatties, cormacks, and daltons. Owlets' eegs (O stoop to please!) are here, creakish from age and all now quite epsilene, and oldwolldy wobblewers, haudworth a wipe o grass. Sss! See the snake wurrums everyside! Our durlbin is sworming in sneaks. They came to our island from triangular Toucheaterre beyond the wet prairie rared up in the midst of the cargon of prohibitive pomefructs but along landed Paddy Wippingham and the his garbagecans cotched the creeps of them pricker than our whosethere outofman could quick up her whatsthats. Somedivide and sumthelot but the tally turns round the same balifuson. Racketeers and bottloggers.

Axe on thwacks on thracks, axenwise. One by one place one by three dittoh and one before. Two nursus one make a plausible free and idim behind. Starting off with a big boaboa and three-legged calvers and ivargraine jadesses with a message in their mouths. And a hundread-filled unleavenweight of liberorumqueue to con an we can till 'allhorrors eve. What a meanderthalltale to unfurl and with what an end in view of squattor and anntisquattor and postproneauntisquattor! To say too us to be every tim, nick and larry of us, sons of the sod, sons, littlesons, yea and lealittlesons, when usses not to be, every sue, siss and sally of us, dugters of Nan! Accusative ahnsire! Damadam to infinities!

True there was in nillohs dieybos as yet no lumpend papeer in the waste and mightmountain Penn still groaned for the micies to let flee. All was of ancientry. You gave me a boot (signs on it!) and I ate the wind. I quizzed you a quid (with for what?) and you went to the quod. But the world, mind, is, was and will be writing its own wrunes for ever, man, on all matters that fall under the ban of our infrarational senses fore the last milchcamel, the heartvein throbbing between his eyebrowns has still to moor before the tomb of his cousin charmian where his date is tethered by the palm that's hers. But the horn, the drinking, the day of dread are not now. A bone, a pebble, a ramskin; chip them, chap them, cut them up allways; leave them to terracook in the muttheringpot:

and Gutenmorg with his cromagnom charter, tintingfast and great primer must once for omniboss step rubrickredd out of the wordpress else is there no virtue more in alcohoran. For that (the rapt one warns) is what papyr is meed of, hides and hints and misses in prints. Till ye finally (though not yet endlike) meet with the acquaintance of

Mister Typus, Mistress Tope and all the little typtopies. Fillstup. So you need hardly spell me how every word will be bound over to carry three score and ten toptypsical readings throughout the book of Doublends Jined (may his forehead be darkened with mud who would sunder!) till Daleth, mahomahouma, who oped it closeth thereof the. Dor.

Cry not yet! There's many a smile to Nondum, with sytty maids per man, sir, and the park's so dark by kindlelight. But look what you have in your handself! The movibles are scrawling in motions, marching, all of them ago, in pit-pat and zingzang for every busy eerie whig's a bit of a torytale to tell. One's upon a thyme and two's behind their lettice leap and three's among the strubbely beds. And the chicks picked their teeths and the dombkey he begay began. You can ask your ass if he believes it. And so cuddy me only wallops have heels.

That one of a wife with folty barnets. For then was the age when hoops ran high. Of a noarch and a chopwife; of a pomme full grave and a fammy of levity; or of golden youths that wanted gelding; or of what the mischievmiss made a man do. Malmarriedad he was reversogassed by the frisque of her frasques and her prytty pyrrhique. Maye faye, she's la gaye this snaky woman! From that trippiery toe expectungpelick! Veil, volantine, valentine eyes. She's the very besch Winnie blows Nay on good. Flou inn, flow ann. Hohore! So it's sure it was her not we! But lay it easy, gentle mien, we are in rearing of a norewhig. So weeny beeny-veenyteeny. Comsy see! Het wis if ee newt. Lissom! lissom! I am doing it. Hark, the corne entreats! And the larpnotes prittle.

It was of a night, late, lang time agone,

in an auldstane eld, when madameen spinning water notty man was every bully ribberrobber that ever everybuddy To his love-billy lived alove with Jarl van Hoother high up in cold hands

Adam was delvin and his silts, when mulk mounty-and the first leal had her ainway saking eyes and every-every biddy else, and had his burnt head his lamphouse, laying on himself.

And his two little jiminies, cousins of ourn, Tristopher and Hilary, were kicka heeling their dummy on the oil cloth flure of his homerigh, castle and earthenhouse. And, be dermot, who come to the keep of his inn only the niece-of-his-in-law, the prankquean. And the prankquean pulled a rosy one and made her wit foreninst the dour. And she lit up and fireland was ablaze. And spoke she to the dour in her petty perusienne:
Mark the Wans, why do I am alook alike a poss of porterpease?
And that was how the skirtmisshes began.

But the dour handworded her grace in dootch nossow: Shut! So her grace o'malice kidsnapped up the jiminy Tristopher and into the shandy westerness she rain, rain, rain. And Jarl van Hoother warlessed after her with soft dovesgall: Stop deef stop come back to my earin stop. But she swaradid to him: Unlikelihud.

And there was a brannewail that same sabboath night of falling angles somewhere in Erio. And the prankquean went for her forty years' walk in Tourlemonde and she washed the blessings of the lovespots off the jiminy with soap sulliver suddles and she had her four owlers masters for to tauch him his tickles and she convorted him to the onesure allgood and he became a luderman.

So then she started to rain and to rain and, be redtom, she was back again at Jarl van Hoother's in a brace of samers and the jiminy with her in her pinafrond, lace at night, at another time. And where did she come but to the bar of his bristolry. And Jarl von Hoother had his baretholobruised heels drowned in his cellarmalt, shaking warm hands with himself and the jiminy Hillary and the dummy in their first infancy were below on the tearsheet, wringing and coughling, like broder and histher. And the prankquean nipped a paly one and lit up again and redcocks flew flackering from the hillcombs. And she made her witter before the wicked, saying: Mark the Twy, why do I am alook alike two poss of porterpease?   And: Shut! says the wicked, handwording her madesty.

So her madesty a forethought set down a jiminy and took up a jiminy and all the lilipath ways to Woeman's Land she rain, rain, rain. And Jarl van Hoother bleethered after her with a loud finegale: Stop domb stop come back with my earring stop.   But the prankquean swaradid: Am liking it. And there was a wild old grannewwall that laurency night of starshootings somewhere in Erio. And the prankquean went for her forty years' walk in Turnlemeem and she punched the curses of cromcruwell with the nail of a top into the jiminy and she had her four larksical monitrix to touch him his tears and she provorted him to the onecertain allsecure and he became a tristian.

So then she started raining, raining, and in a pair of changers, be dom ter, she was back again at Jarl von Hoother's and the Larryhill with her under her abromette. And why would she halt at all if not by the ward of his mansionhome of another nice lace for the third charm? And Jarl von Hoother had his hurricane hips up to his pantrybox, ruminating in his holdfour stomachs, (Dare! O dare!), and the jiminy Toughertrees and the dummy were belove on the watercloth, kissing and spitting, and roghuing and poghuing, like knavepaltry and naivebride and in their second infancy. And the prankquean picked a blank and lit out and the valleys lay twinkling. And she made her wittest in front of the arkway of trihump, asking:

Mark the Tris, why do I am alook alike three poss of porter pease?

But that was how the skirtmishes endupped.

For like the campbells acoming with a fork lance
of lightning, Jarl von Hoother Boanerges himself,
the old terror of the dames, came hip hop handihap
out through the pikeopened arkway of his three shut-
tonned castles, in his broadginger hat and his civic
chollar and his allabuff hemmed and his bullbraggin
soxangloves and his ladbroke breeks and his cattegut
bandolair and his furframed panuncular cumbottes
like a rud yellan gruebleen orangeman in his violet
indignation, to the whole longth of the strongth of
his bowman's bill. And he clopped his rude hand
to his eacy hitch and he ordurd and his thick
spch spck for her to

shut up shop, dappy.

And the duppy shot the shutter clup

(PERKOD-
HUS KURUN-
BARG GRUAUYA-
GOK GORLAYOR-
GROMGREMMIT-
GHUNDHURTHRUMA-
THUNARADI DILLI-
FAITITILLI BUMULLU-
NUKKUNUN !)

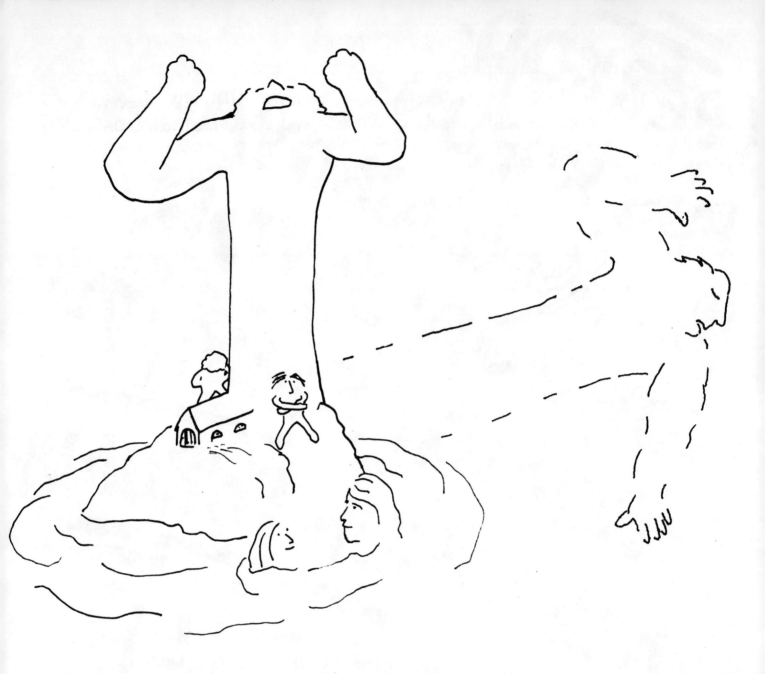

And they all drank free. For one man in his armour was a fat match always for any girls under shurts. And that was the first peace of illiterative porthery in all the flamend floody flatuous world. How kirssy the tiler made a sweet unclose to the Narwhealian captol. Saw fore shalt thou sea. Betoun ye and be. The prankquean was to hold her dummy ship and the jimminies was to keep the peacewave and van Hoother was to git the wind up. Thus the hearsomeness of the burger felicitates the whole of the polis.

O foenix culprit!

Ex nickylow malo comes mickelmassed bonum. Hill, rill, ones in company, billeted, less be proud of. Breast high and bestride! Only for that these will not breathe upon Norronesen or Irenean the secrest of their soorcelossness. Quarry silex, Homfrie Noanswa!

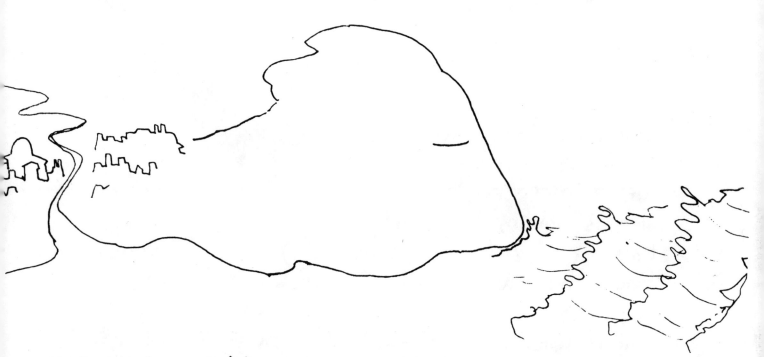

Undy gentian festyknees, Livia Noanswa?

Wolkencap is on him, frowned; audiurient, he would evesdrip, were it mous at hand, were it dinn of bottles in the far ear. Murk, his vales are darkling. With lipth she lithpeth to him all to time of thuch on thuch and thow on thow. She he she ho she ha to la. Hairfluke, if he could bad twig her! Impalpabunt, he abhears. The soundwaves are his buffeteers; they trompe him with their trompes; the wave of roary and the wave of hooshed and the wave of hawhaw hawrd and the wave of neverheedthemhorseluggarsandlistletomine. Landloughed by his neighboor-mistress and perpetrified in his offsprung sabes and suckers, the moaning pipers could tell him to his faceback, the louthly one whose loab we are devorers of, how butt for his hold halibutt, or her to her pudor puff, the lipalip one whose libe we drink at, how biff for her tiddywink of a windfall, our breed and washer givers, there would not be a holey spier on the town nor a vestal flouting in the dock, nay to make plein avowels, nor a yew nor an eye to play cash cash in Novo Nilbud by swamplight nor a' toole o' tall o' toll and noddy hint to the convaynience.

He dug in an dug out
by the skill of his tilth for himself
and all belonging to him and he
sweated his crew beneath his
auspice for the living and he
urned his dread, that
dragon volant, and
he made louse for us
and delivered us to boll
weevils amain, that mighty
liberator, Unfru-Chikda-Oru-Wukru and
begad he did, our ancestor most worshipful, til he thought
of a better one in his windower's house with that blush-
mantle upon him from earsend to earsend. And would
again could whispring grassies wake him and may again
when the fiery bird disembers. And will again if so be
sooth by elders to his youngers shall be said. Have you
whines for my wedding, did you bring bride and bedding,
will you whoop for my deading is a ? Wake?

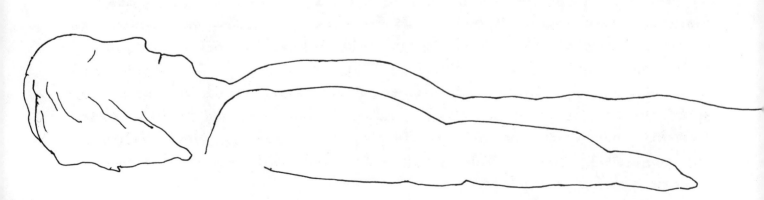

Usqueadbaugham!

Anam muck an dhoul! Did ye drink me doornail?

Now be aisy, good Mr Finnimore, sir.
And take your laysure like a god on pension and don't be walking abroad Sure you'd only lose yourself in Healiopolis now the way your roads in Kapelavaster are that winding there after the calvary, the North Umbrian and the Fivs Barrow and Waddlings Raid and the Bower Moore and wet your feet maybe with the foggy dew's abroad. Meeting some sick old bankrupt or the Cottericks' donkey with his shoe hanging, clankata chankata, or a slut snoring with an impure infant on a bench. 'Twould turn you against life, so 'twould. And the weather's that mean too. To part from Devlin is hard as Nugent knew, to leave the clean tanglesome one lushier than its neighbour enfranchisable fields but let your ghost have no grievance.

You're better off, sir, where you are, primesigned in the full of your dress, bloodeagle waistcoat and all, remembering your shapes and sizes on the pillow of your babycurls under your sycamore by the keld water where the Tory's clay will scare the varmints and have all you want, pouch, gloves, flask, bricket, kerchief, ring and amberulla, the whole treasure of the pyre, in the land of souls with Homin and Broin Baroke and pole old Lonan and Nobucketnozzler and the Guinnghis Khan. And we'll be coming here the ombre players, to rake your gravel and bringing you presents, won't we, fenians? And it isn't our spittle we'll stint you of, is it, druids? Not shabbty little imagettes, penny-dirts and dodgemyeyes you buy in the soottee stores. But offerings of the field. Mieliodories, that Doctor Faherty, the madison man, taught to gooden you. Poppypap's a passport out. And honey's the holiest thing ever was, hive, comb and earwax, the food for glory, (mind you keep the pot or your nectar cup may yield too light!) and some goat's milk, sir, like the maid used to bring you.

Your fame is spreading like Basilico's ointment since the Fintan Ialors piped you overborder and there's whole household's beyond the Bothnians and they calling names after you. The men here's always talking of you sitting around on the pig's cheeks under the sacred rooftree, over the bowls of memory where every hollow holds a hallow, with a pledge to the drengs, in the Salmon House.

And admiring to our supershillelagh where the palmsweat on high is the mark of your manument. All the toethpicks ever Eirenesians chewed on are chips chepped from that battery block. If you were bowed and soild and letdown itself from the oner of the load it was that paddyplanters might pack up plenty and when you were undone in every point fore the laps of goddesses you showed our labour-lasses how to free was easy. The game old Gunne, they do be saying, (skull!) that was a planter for you, a spicer of them all. Begog but he was, G.O.G! He's duddandgunne now and we're apter finding the sores of his sedeq but peace to his great limbs, the buddhoch, with the last league long rest of him, while the millioncandled eye of Tuskar sweeps the Moylean Main! There was never a warlord in Great Erinnes and Brettland, no, nor in all Pike County like you, they say. No, nor a king nor an ardking, bung king, sung king or hung king. That you could fell an elmstree twelve urchins couldn't ring round and hoist high the stone that Liam failed. Who but a Maccullaghmore the reise of our fortunes and the faunayman at the funeral to compass our cause? If you was hogglebully itself and most frifty like you was taken waters still what all where was your like to lay the cable or who was the batter could better Your Grace? Mick Mac Magnus MacCawley can take you off to the pure perfection and Leatherbags Reynolds tries your shuffle and cut. But as Hopkins and Hopkins puts it, you were the pale eggynaggy and a kis to tilly up. We calls him the Buggaloffs since he went Jerusalemfaring in Arssia Manor. You had a gamier cock than Pete, Jake or Martin and your archgoose of geese stubbled for All Angels' Day. So may the priest of seven worms and scalding tayboil, Papa Vestray, come never anear you as your hair grows wheater beside the Liffey that's in Heaven!

Hep, hep, hurrah there!
Hero!
Seven times thereto we salute you!

The whole bag of kits, falcon plumes and jackbotes incloted, is where you flung them that time. Your heart is in the system of the Shewolf and your crested head is in the tropic of Capricapron. Your feet are in the cloister of Virgo. Your olala is in the region of sahuls. And that's ashore as you were born. Your shuck ticks swell. And that there texas is tow linen. The loamsome roam to Laffayette is ended. Drop in your tracks, babe! Be not unrested! The headboddylwatcher of the chempel of Isid, Totum calmum, saith: I know thee, metherjar, I know thee, thou abramanation, who comest ever without thee, being invoked, whose coming is unknown, all the things which the company of the precentors and of the grammarians of Christpatrick's ordered concerning thee in the matter of thy tombing. Howe of the shipmen, steep wall!

Everything's going on the same or so it appeals to all of us, in the old holmsted here. Coughings all over the sanctuary, bad scrant to me aunt Florenza. The horn for breakfast, one o'gong for lunch and dinnerchime. As popular as when Belly the First was keng and his members met in the Diet of Man. The same shop slop in the window. Jacob's lettercrackers and Dr Tipple's Vi-Cocoa and the Eswuards' dessippated soup beside Mother Seagull's syrup. Meat took a drop when Reilly-Parsons failed. Coal's short but we've plenty of bog in the yard. And barley's up again, begrained to it. The lads is attending school nessans regular, sir, spelling, beesknees with hathatansy and turning out tables by mudapplication. Allfor the books and never pegging smashers after Tom Bowe Glassarse or Timmy the Tosser. 'Tisraely the truth! No, isn't it, roman pathoricks?

You were the doublejoynted janitor the morning they were delivered and you'll be a grandfer yet entirely when the ritehand seizes what the lovearm knows. Kevin's just a doat with his cherub cheek, chalking oghres on walls, and his little lamp and schoolbelt and bag of knicks, playing postman's knock round the diggings and if the seep were milk you could lieve his olde by his ide but, laus sake, the devil does be in that knirps of a Jerry sometimes, the tarandtan plaidboy, making encostive inkum out of the last of his lavings and writing a blue streak over his bourseday shirt. Hetty Jane's a child of Mary. She'll be coming (for they're sure to choose her) in her white of gold with a tourch of ivy to rekindle the flame on Felix Day. But Essie Shanahan has let down her skirts. You remember Essie in our Luna's Convent? They called her Holly Merry her lips were so ruddyberry and Pia de Purebelle when the redminers riots was on about her. Were I a clerk designate to the Williams-woodsmenufactors I'd poster those pouters on every jamb in the town. She's making her rep at Lanner's twicenightly. With the tabarine tamtammers of the whirligigmagees. Beats that cachucha flat. 'Twould dilate your heart to go.

Aisy now, you decent man, with your knees
and lie quiet and repose your honour's lordship!
Hold him here, Ezekiel Irons, and may God strengthen
you! It's our warm spirits, boys, he's spooring.
Dimitrius O'Flagonan, cork that cure for the Clan-
cartys! You swamped enough since Portobello to
float the Pomeroy. Fetch neahere, Pat Koy! And fetch
nouyou, Pam Yates! Be nayther angst of Wramawitch!
Here's lumbos. Where misties swaddlum, where misches
lodge none, where mystries pour kind on, O sleepy!
So be yet!

I've an eye on queer Behan and old Kate and the butter, trust me. She'll do no jugglywuggly with her war souvenir postcards to help to build me murial, tippers! I'll trip your traps! Assure a sure there! And we put on your clock again, sir, for you. Did

or didn't we, sharestutterers? So you won't be up a stump entirely. Nor shed your remnants. The sternwheel's strong. Hold your missus. Like the crawling I seen in the queenoveire. Arrah, it's herself that's talking! fine, too, don't be talking! You storyan grass woman plelthy good trout. Shakeshands. Dibble a hayfork's wrong with her only her lex's salig. Boald Tib does be yawning and smirking cat's hours on the Pollockses' woolly round tabouretcushion watching her sewing a dream together, the tailor's daughter, stitch to her last. Or while waiting for winter to fire the enchantement, decoying more nesters to fall down the flue. It's an allavalonche that blows nopussy food. If you only were there to explain the meaning, best of men, and talk to her nice of guldensilver. The lips would moisten once again.

As when you drove with her to Findrinny
Fair. What with reins here and ribbons
there all your hands were employed so she
never knew was she on land or at sea
or swooped through the blue like Airwinger's
bride. She was flirtsome then and she's
fluttersome yet. She can second a song
and adores a scandal when the last post's
gone by. Fond of a concertina and pair's
passing when she's had her forty winks
for supper after kanekannan and abbely dimpling
and is in her merlin chair assotted, reading
her Evening World.

To see is it smarts, full lengths or swaggers. News, news, all the news. Death, a leopard, kills fellah in Fez. Angry scenes at Stormount. Stilla Star with her lucky in goingaways. Opportunity fair with the China floods and we here these rosy rumours. Ding Tams he noise about all some Harry chap. She's seeking her way, a chickle a chuckle, in and out of their serial story, *Les Loves of Selskar et Pervenche*, freely adapted to *The Novvergins Viv*. There'll be bluebells blowing in salty sepulchres the night she signs her final tear. Zee End. But that's a world of ways away. Till track laws time. No silver ash or switches for that one! While flattering candles flare. Anna Stacey's how are you! Worther waist in the noblest, says Adams and Sons, the wouldpay actionneers. Her hair's as brown as ever it was. And wivvy and wavy. Repose you now! Finn no more!

For, be that samesake sibsubstitute of a hooky salmon, there's already a big rody ram lad at random on the premises of his haunt of the hungred bordles, as it is told me. Shop Illicit, flourishing like a lord-major or a buaboabaybohm, litting flop a deadlop (aloose!) to lee but lifting a bennbranch a yardalong (ivoeh!) on the breezy side (for showm!), the height of Brewster's chimpney and as broad below as Phineas Barnum; humphing his share of the showthers is senken on him he's such a grandfallar, with a pocked wife in pickle that's a flyfire and three lice nittle clinkers, two twilling bugs and one midgit pucelle. And aither he cursed and recursed and was everseen doing what your fourfootlers saw or he was never done seeing what you coolpigeons know, weep the clouds aboon for smiledown witnesses, and that'll do now about the fairyhees and frailyshees.

Though Eset fibble it to the zephiroth and Artsa zoom it round her heavens for ever. Creator he has created for his creatured ones a creation. White mono-thoid? Red theatrocrat? And all the pinkprophets cohalething? Very much so! But however 'twas 'tis sure for one thing, what sherif Toragh voucherfors and Mapquiq makes put out, that the man, Humme the Cheapner, Esc, overseen as we thought him, yet a worthy of the naym, came at this timecoloured place where we live in our paroqial fermament one tide on another, with a bumrush in a hull of a wherry, the twin turbane dhow, *The Bay for Dybbling*, this archipelago's first visiting schooner, with a wicklowpattern waxenwench at her prow for a figurehead, the deadsea dugong updip-dripping from his depths,

and has been repreaching himself like a
fishmummer these siktyten years ever since,
his shebi by his shide, adi and aid, growing
hoarish under his turban and changing cane
sugar into sethulose starch (Tuttut's cess to him!)
as also that, batin the bulkihood he bloats about
when innebbiated, our old offender was humile,
commune and ensectuous from his nature,
which you may gauge after the bynames was
put under him, in lashons of languages, (honnein
suit and praisers be!) and, totalisating him, even
hamissin of himashim that he, sober serious,
he is ee and no counter he who will be
ultimendly respunchable for the hubbub caused
in Edenborough.